WHEN A PHANTOM
SPAWNS

WHEN A PHANTOM
SPAWNS

AQUATIC ADVENTURES
IN THE OVERWORLD

BOOK ONE

AN UNOFFICIAL
MINECRAFTERS NOVEL

MAGGIE MARKS

Sky Pony Press
New York

Sky Pony Press books may be purchased in bulk at special discounts for
sales promotion, corporate gifts, fund-raising, or educational purposes.
Special editions can also be created to specifications. For details, contact
the Special Sales Department, Sky Pony Press, 307 West 36th Street,
11th Floor, New York, NY 10018 or info@skyhorsepublishing.com.

Sky Pony® is a registered trademark of Skyhorse Publishing, Inc.®,
a Delaware corporation.

Visit our website at www.skyponypress.com.

10 9 8 7 6 5 4 3 2 1

Library of Congress Cataloging-in-Publication Data is available on file.

Special thanks to Erin L. Falligant.

Cover illustration by Amanda Brack
Cover design by Brian Peterson

Hardcover ISBN: 978-1-5107-4726-5
E-book ISBN: 978-1-5107-4737-1

Printed in the United States of America

TABLE OF CONTENTS

CHAPTER 1 1
CHAPTER 2 11
CHAPTER 3 19
CHAPTER 4 25
CHAPTER 5 31
CHAPTER 6 39
CHAPTER 7 47
CHAPTER 8 53
CHAPTER 9 59
CHAPTER 10 65
CHAPTER 11 73
CHAPTER 12 81
CHAPTER 13 87
CHAPTER 14 93
CHAPTER 15 99

WHEN A PHANTOM SPAWNS

CHAPTER 1

Hang on!" Uncle Bart hollered from the ship's wheel. His words were swallowed up by the gusty wind and rain.

Mason gripped the rail, fighting to keep his footing on the slick wet deck. Below, fierce waves swirled around the hull of the ship. Around and around like a whirlpool, the waves tugged at the boat, as if trying to suck it downward to the ocean floor.

Beneath Mason's feet, the boat shook and shuddered. The sea tugged it in one direction. Uncle Bart braced the wheel, forcing the boat in another. Mason stared at the dark oak planks beneath his feet. Would the ship split in two?

And where was Asher? Mason spun his head, searching the deck for his little brother. He called out for him, choking on rainwater. "Asher!" He listened for a response, but heard only the rumble of thunder overhead.

Gripping the rail, Mason staggered toward the bow of the ship. Step by step, he kept his head down, braced *against the thrashing wind. When he had nearly reached his uncle, he felt the ship shift sideways.*

The deck slid out from beneath Mason's feet. He tumbled and slid, grasping desperately for something—anything—to hold on to. As he crashed into the base of the thick wooden mast, he grabbed on tight.

Mason struggled to right himself, just as a crack of lightning split the night sky. There was Uncle Bart, silhouetted in blinding light. He hung from the deck rail, his feet dangling as the ship toppled sideways. Mason watched in horror as his uncle lost his grip . . . and plunged toward the raging water below.

Mason woke with a start. He sucked in his breath and sat up straight, squinting into the sun that sunk low in the western sky.

Just a dream, he told himself. He relaxed into a stretch.

But when he wiped the sleep from his eyes, he could see more clearly. He was sitting on the deck of a ship. As he stood, he saw sand stretching out for miles to his left. And to his right? Ocean waters, calmer now but vast—nothing but blue for as far as the eye could see.

Reality hit Mason like a punch to the gut. The storm *wasn't* just a dream. It had actually happened—every horrifying moment. The ship had overturned. And Uncle Bart had fallen into the fierce waves and . . . disappeared.

Mason slid his finger across the notches carved into the rail of the ship. He and Asher had carved one for every day that had passed since the storm.

Three days since the boat had been sucked into a whirlpool.

Three days since the boys had been shipwrecked on shore.

Three days since they had last seen Uncle Bart.

Mason fought the urge to sink back down to the deck and curl up into a ball. But he couldn't. He had to look out for his brother. Had Asher been sleeping, too?

Mason spun in a slow circle, searching the deck. "Asher!"

A fishing pole waved in the air near the stern of the boat. Mason hurried along the deck until he could see Asher's shock of red hair. His brother was fishing off the stern, which was close to the water now that the tide had rolled in.

"Catch anything?" Mason called.

Asher shook his head. "Only a few fish. I tossed them back."

Mason threw up his hands. "Why did you toss them back? We're running low on food, remember?"

Asher shot him a disgusted look. "I don't eat fish! Gross. You know that."

Mason counted to five before answering—a trick he used whenever Asher was driving him crazy. *One, two, three, four . . . oh, forget it.* "So why are you fishing if you don't want to catch fish?" Mason snapped.

Asher shrugged. "I'm fishing for treasure. Uncle Bart says I might catch a nautilus shell, or maybe an enchanted book."

Uncle Bart, thought Mason, remembering again

the moment when his uncle had been swept off the deck. He squeezed his eyes shut, trying to erase the memory. Then he opened them and glanced at Asher, who was the spitting image of their uncle. Red hair. Pale skin. Freckles. And that gleam in his eye whenever the word *treasure* came up.

We wouldn't even be in this mess if Uncle Bart hadn't been searching for buried treasure, Mason thought bitterly.

But now Uncle Bart was gone. And Asher was acting as if it were just another day, another treasure hunt. As if Uncle Bart would come jogging along the beach any minute now to say that he'd found some loot and that it was time to set sail for home.

"We don't need nautilus shells," said Mason, trying to keep his voice steady. "But if you want to do something useful, you could help me patch the holes in the hull."

Asher snorted. "Useful? You were just napping for like three hours. What's so useful about sleeping all the time?"

"I don't sleep—" Mason started to say. *I don't sleep anymore. Not a wink. Not since a creeper blew holes in the hull of our ship. Not since I've had to spend my nights wide awake, standing guard on deck—guarding YOU.*

But he didn't say any of that. What good would it do? Instead, he hopped to his feet and started pacing, which always helped him think. "We have to make a plan," he told Asher. "It's been three days, and we have to figure out what we're going to do next."

Asher glanced up. "You're going to wear a hole in the deck from pacing," he said with a crooked smile. "That's pretty much what you're going to do next."

"There are already holes," said Mason. "Take a look around."

In the fading sunlight, the ship looked especially tattered. Planks of wood stuck up every which way along the deck. The rail had snapped in half near the bow of the ship. And the sail had been stripped from its mast. Nothing flew overhead except a pirate flag that Asher had raised—to make the shipwreck look "tougher," he'd said.

"This ship won't sail again," declared Mason. "We need to move on. Maybe we can take the rowboat across the water back to the mainland."

Both boys turned toward the rowboat that hung from the deck rail. It was so tiny. And the ocean? The waves looked choppier now against the setting sun. *We'd never make it,* thought Mason. His stomach sunk.

"We can't leave Uncle Bart," said Asher, sticking out his chin. "What if he comes back and we're gone?"

"He's not coming back." The harsh words slipped out of Mason's mouth before he could stop them.

"He is!" argued Asher.

Mason crouched beside his brother, staring him right in the eye. "He was swept off the deck, Asher. I saw it happen. There's no way he survived the storm." He fought down the lump in his throat.

"He *did* survive," Asher said firmly. "And I'll tell you why." He counted off the reasons on his fingers.

"First, he had his helmet on, enchanted with respiration. He can breathe underwater. Also, he was wearing his Depth Strider boots. He can swim faster than any fish in the sea. And he knows the ocean. He has a map, remember?"

Mason wanted to point out that enchantments don't last that long—not for three days. But Asher's cheeks were flaming red now, so he stayed silent.

"Plus, Uncle Bart had his buried treasure map. He always carried that with him."

Mason nodded. He could picture the map, too—folded in quarters. His uncle had opened and closed it so many times, the map had practically torn in two.

Asher's eyes lit up. "He's probably hunting for buried treasure right now. Maybe he already found the Heart of the Sea!" He jumped to his feet and peered out over the deck rail, as if Uncle Bart might pop up out of the waves any second now.

Heart of the Sea, thought Mason, shaking his head. It was all Uncle Bart had talked about for weeks. Forget emeralds, diamonds, and gold. All he wanted was the rare Heart of the Sea, to build a conduit so he could safely explore the ocean's floor.

With a conduit, they could breathe underwater, see more easily, and mine more quickly. *But Uncle Bart will never craft it now,* thought Mason, his stomach clenching. *And he's not coming back for us. We're on our own— just like before.*

Just like when their parents had been killed in a mining accident. That's when Uncle Bart had taken the boys in, and started bringing them along on his ocean adventures. For a while, they had felt like a real family. *But not anymore,* thought Mason.

As he stood beside Asher on the deck of the wrecked ship, he felt as if they were the last two kids in the entire Overworld. He threw his arm around Asher's shoulders. "Time to eat," he said. "And then bed."

The sun dipped so low in the sky now, shadows spilled across the deck. That meant mobs would spawn soon.

And I'll have another sleepless night, thought Mason with a sigh.

* * *

Mason pulled his head out of the supply chest and frowned. "Limp carrots, wrinkly potatoes, or mushroom stew. Which sounds better?"

"Um, stew," said Asher. "Definitely stew."

They'd eaten nothing but stew for the last few days. But as Mason pulled the stew from the chest, he took a whiff. Something smelled off—almost sweet, like flowers. He shook his head and put it back. "Nope. Smells suspicious."

"It's fine!" said Asher. "C'mon, I'm hungry."

"It could be poisonous," said Mason. "I've heard about people going *blind* from eating suspicious stew."

Asher snorted. "You made that up."

But Mason had already put some withered carrots and potatoes into the furnace. "It's roasted vegetables tonight," he said firmly. "Unless you want to catch us some fish."

Asher's face practically turned green. "I just lost my appetite."

But a few minutes later, he gobbled down those roasted vegetables as if he hadn't eaten in a week. Mason slid one more potato onto his brother's plate, even though his own stomach grumbled.

As darkness fell, Mason's eyelids grew heavy. But he'd made only one bed of blankets on the deck of the ship. As he hung a brightly lit torch on the wooden mast, he pointed to the blankets. "You sleep," he told Asher. "I'll keep watch."

By the time Asher had climbed into the bed, Mason had armed his bow. Mobs could already be spawning on the beach below. He had to be ready.

But the bow was so heavy! As Mason's arms grew weak with sleepiness, the bow sunk lower into his lap. The last thing he remembered was studying the loopy letter *B*—Uncle Bart's initial engraved into the bow. Then Mason's eyelids closed and his head fell backward, hitting the mast with a thud.

That's when something swooped down from overhead.

He heard the *whoosh* of wings. Something grazed his hair. Bats?

Mason's eyes flew open.

For a moment, he was blinded by the light of the torch. As his eyes adjusted, he spotted the shadowy creature swirling overhead—no, two of them. Maybe three.

The winged creatures circled the mast, swooping lower and lower. But these weren't bats. No, they were much, *much* larger.

As one dipped low, Mason saw green, glowing eyes.

He heard the growl of the undead mob.

And he came face to face with . . . a *phantom*.

CHAPTER 2

Mason raised his bow, but it was too late. The mob was too close!

As the winged phantom swooped toward his face, nipping at his skin, Mason swung his bow. *Smack!* The creature darted away.

As it flew back into the night sky, Mason aimed his bow and released an arrow. *Thwack!* The arrow hit its mark. The phantom grunted, glowed blood red, and tumbled toward the beach below.

Mason didn't look to see where it had landed or whether it was coming back. He grabbed Asher's arm. "Wake up! Get up!"

"What?" Asher struggled to break free.

"Phantoms!" Mason cried. "We have to get below deck!"

As he half-carried, half-dragged his brother toward the staircase, more winged mobs circled overhead. As another phantom swooped down, Mason flung his arm, clipping the creature's fleshy wing. Then he dove for the stairs, taking Asher tumbling down with him.

When they reached the cabin, moonlight spilled in through the cracks in the hull. Mason crawled toward the largest crack and peered outside. Shadows of the phantoms still circled the beach. They dipped and darted, searching for their prey. *Searching for us,* thought Mason with horror.

"What are they?" cried Asher. He was wide awake now, his hair sticking up in wayward tufts.

"Phantoms," Mason whispered, as if the mobs might hear. "They'll burn up in daylight, but . . . " He checked the night sky. "That's hours from now."

When he saw the terror in Asher's green eyes, he steeled his voice. "They can't get us down here," he promised. *But in this dark cabin, other mobs can,* he instantly realized.

He lit a torch and pulled Asher into the light. "Stay against the wall. I'll guard the door—er, the crack."

For once, Asher did as he was told.

Minutes passed like hours as the brothers waited. Asher's head began to bob against the wall. When Mason checked again, his brother was fast asleep.

But I'm pretty sure I'll never sleep again, thought Mason. He got to his feet in the shadowy cabin and began to pace the floor.

* * *

"Hey, there!"

Mason woke to the sound of a girl's voice. He'd been sleeping sitting up, his head propped against the splintered wood of the cabin wall. He wiped the drool from his chin and leaped to his feet, reaching out to steady himself. "Who . . . who's there?" he stammered.

As he stepped out of the cracked hull, sunlight blinded him. But sunlight meant no more phantoms. No more undead mobs. Only a girl, *somewhere*. Or had he dreamed her?

Mason searched the beach that led to the water.

"Hello, little fella," the girl's voice rang out, clear as a bell.

Mason whirled around and saw a dark-haired girl crouched low in the sand. She held a handful of seagrass. But she wasn't talking to him. She was speaking to something on the ground. A critter, maybe?

"Hey!" Mason's heart leaped at the sight of another human being. He stumbled toward her across the uneven sand.

She glanced up, her eyes wide. "Stop!"

Huh? Mason froze.

"Don't hurt them!"

"Hurt who?" Mason glanced right and then left. But they were the only two people on the beach, as far as he could see.

"The baby turtles!" The girl pointed at the tiny creatures scuttling through the sand.

Mason squatted low for a closer look.

"The eggs just hatched," said the girl. "Four of them. We have to help them get out to sea, before a drowned or some other mob comes and stomps on them." She waved the seagrass in front of another baby turtle, as if coaxing it toward the water.

Mason suddenly wished he had a handful of grass, too. "Why don't we just pick them up?" he asked.

She shot him a horrified look. "Don't you know anything about turtles? Don't touch them. Just do what I tell you to do."

For some reason, Mason did. Whoever this girl was, she seemed to know a whole lot about turtles. So Mason stepped aside as she led her baby sea turtle parade toward the water.

She didn't speak again until all four babies were taking their first swim. Then she brushed the sand and grass off her fingers, put her hands on her hips, and cast him a satisfied smile. "See?"

He nodded. "But who are you?" he blurted. "Where did you come from?"

She shrugged. "Around. The real question is, where did *you* come from?" She waved at the wrecked ship. "Are your parents on deck?"

Mason's mouth suddenly felt dry. He shook his head. "It's just me and my brother." He searched her face for surprise, and waited for her to ask him what had become of his parents. But she didn't.

"Can I see the ship?" she asked.

Who is this girl, anyway? thought Mason. She seemed so bold—showing up from out of nowhere and then asking for a tour of the ship, without even telling Mason her name. Irritation pricked at his chest. "Tell me your name first," he said, stepping forward to block her path.

She smiled at him, or maybe it was a smirk. "Luna," she finally said. "Like *lunar*—the moon."

He nodded. At least it was a start. "I'm Mason," he said. "And my brother Asher is still sleeping."

"Because of the phantoms?" she asked.

Mason sucked in his breath, remembering. He glanced upward, as if one of the winged creatures might appear. But the sun shone bright. Any phantoms that had still been here by morning's light had burned to a crisp. "How'd you know about them?" he asked Luna.

She shrugged. "One of them dropped a membrane." She picked up a stick and carefully lifted the thin, see-through membrane from the sand. "When a phantom spawns, you know you've been awake too long." She gave Mason a knowing look.

"Who's been awake too long?" Asher stepped out of the hull of the ship, rubbing his eyes.

Luna laughed out loud. "Not you, sleepy head."

She talked to him as if she'd known him forever, which annoyed Mason all over again.

Asher glanced up at Luna. "Who are you?" he asked. "Did Uncle Bart send you?"

She shook her head. "Who's Uncle Bart?"

Asher started yammering away, as if Uncle Bart were his favorite topic. "He's a treasure hunter. He's searching for buried treasure right now—he has a map, and a helmet enchanted with respiration. And when he finds the treasure, he's going to come back for us."

Luna glanced at Mason, studying his face with her curious brown eyes. But Mason shook his head. Uncle Bart wasn't coming back, no matter how much Asher wanted it to be true.

"I have a buried treasure map, too," said Luna brightly.

Asher perked right up. "You do? Can I see it?"

"It's at my house," said Luna. "You could follow me. I'll show you." She pointed toward the water, as if a ship might suddenly appear to take her home.

Mason searched the horizon, but the waves seemed endless and empty. "Where do you live?" he asked.

This time, Luna answered him directly. "In the sea," she said simply.

"On an island?" piped up Asher.

She shook her head. "Underwater."

As Asher's eyes widened, Mason blew out his breath. "She's joking, Asher. Don't get too excited."

Luna's face darkened. "I'm telling the truth," she said. "I live underwater. I'll show you, if you're up for the swim."

"I am!" Asher headed toward the water, ready to dive into the waves.

"Asher, *stop*!" Even Mason was surprised by the force of his words. "We're not following someone we don't know into the sea—without a boat or an enchanted helmet or *anything*. What's wrong with you?"

Asher scowled, as if Mason had just stolen his treasure chest.

Luna shrugged. "Suit yourself." She turned on her heel, without a goodbye, and strode past Asher.

She walked straight into those waves, until they were waist high.

Then she dove underwater. And disappeared.

CHAPTER 3

"Fine. Then I'll go without you." Asher crossed his arms and kicked at the deck with his sneaker.

He'd been grumpy all day, ever since Luna had disappeared—as if Mason had kept him from some great adventure.

"How?" Mason shot back. "How are you going to go without me? You're not the Overworld's best swimmer. And Uncle Bart took his enchanted armor with him."

Asher shrugged. "Luna didn't need armor. So maybe I don't either."

Mason remembered the moment when Luna had disappeared under the waves. How had she done that? Where had she gone? He was as curious as Asher, but he couldn't let his brother see that. Asher was apt to dive off the deck of the ship and go after her.

"Let's fish instead," Mason said, changing the subject. "If you catch some cod, I'll cook it up. It'll taste just like chicken."

Asher puffed out his cheeks, as if Mason had suggested eating rotten flesh. "I don't like fish. It's disgusting—I told you that!"

"Well, maybe you'll get lucky and catch yourself a nautilus shell." Mason watched his brother's face, hoping he'd take the bait. But he didn't.

"You never want to do anything fun," said Asher. "Uncle Bart is fun. He would have gone swimming with Luna."

Mason couldn't argue with that. Uncle Bart would have been the first one to dive in. "Well, he's not here," said Mason. "And it's my job to look out for you. So we're not going in the water without a boat. And we're eating *fish* for dinner."

As Mason reached for the fishing pole, Asher pushed himself up from the deck and brushed past him. Mason heard the thud of Asher's footsteps on the steps leading down to the cabin.

Fine, thought Mason. *I'll fish without you.*

But as he cast his line, he listened. It was way too quiet below deck. What was Asher doing? Worry nibbled at Mason's insides, like a fish nipping at a hook. Finally, he set down the pole and hurried downstairs.

He smelled mushrooms before he had even rounded the corner into the supply room. *No, not the suspicious stew . . .*

Sure enough, Asher had warmed up a bowl of the foul-smelling stuff. He shoved a spoon into the bowl and raised a heaping mound of stew toward his mouth.

"No!" cried Mason. "That's rotten—it could be poisonous!"

But Asher took a noisy slurp. He licked his lips, and smiled. "I think it's delicious." Then he lifted the bowl to his mouth and drank the whole thing down.

* * *

"Do you feel sick?" Mason asked again. He'd been pacing the floor of the supply room, stopping every few seconds to inspect his brother's face. "Can you see my hand? How many fingers am I holding up?" He wiggled his fingers until Asher swatted them away.

"I'm fine!" Asher snapped. "Don't be dumb. It was just stew." Then his expression shifted. He jumped up from his chair so suddenly, it toppled backward. Then he raced out of the room and up the stairs to the deck.

"Asher!" As Mason sprinted after his brother, his heart pounded in his ears. Was Asher going to be sick? Or . . . worse?

He expected Asher to race toward the deck—to hurl the contents of his stomach into the water below. But he didn't. He raced *around* the deck, faster than Mason had ever seen him run. "Asher, wait up!"

He made four laps around the deck in record time. Then he collapsed into a heap, breathing hard and laughing hysterically. "That was so fun!"

Mason dropped to his knees beside his brother. "Are you okay? What just happened?"

Asher shrugged. "I don't know." He wiped the

sweat off his forehead. "Maybe sometimes suspicious stew makes you sick. And maybe other times, it gives you super powers, like speed."

Mason cocked his head. "Maybe you're right." Asher might as well have drunk a potion of swiftness.

"See?" said Asher, a triumphant look spreading across his face. "Sometimes when you take a risk and try something fun, good things happen." He pushed himself up and headed toward the deck rail. "So if Luna comes back today," he called over his shoulder, "I'm going with her."

Mason sighed. *If Luna comes back, we'll both be going with her*, he realized. *Because there's no stopping Asher now.*

Except Luna didn't come back.

That night, after Mason cooked up the very last wrinkly potato from the supply chest, he cast his line into the water, hoping for fish.

But a part of him was hoping for Luna's dark head to pop out of the water instead. Because if she really did live nearby, maybe there was a place to find food and to keep Asher safe.

But how can a girl live underwater? Mason wondered, staring into the dark waters. *How can she survive?*

As night fell, his hopes did, too. Because nighttime meant phantoms in the sky. And mobs spawning on the beach, threatening to creep and stagger into the cracked hull of the boat.

How will we *survive?* Mason wondered. Without food or sleep, he couldn't protect Asher for much longer.

He reeled in his line, set the fishing pole aside, and reached for his bow and arrow instead.

* * *

Morning brought vivid dreams of fighting the drowned—zombies that live deep underwater. They tugged at Mason's arms and legs, pulling him toward his watery death. He yanked his arm back, shrieked, and opened his eyes to find . . .

. . . Asher tugging him awake. "She's here!" his brother cried.

"Who?" Mason slapped his hand against his chest, wishing his heart would stop racing.

"Luna!"

Mason leaped to his feet. He followed Asher out of the cracked hull onto the beach.

Luna wasn't talking to baby turtles today, but she was holding turtle shells—two of them. She held one out to Asher.

"You can wear it like a helmet," she said. "It'll help you breathe underwater, at least for a little while."

Asher took the turtle shell without question and plopped it on his head. "Cool!"

But when Luna offered one to Mason, he froze. If he put on the helmet, would she make them follow her underwater? "How far away is your, um, house?" he asked.

She shrugged. "Not far. You don't have to come. I just thought you might want to see my buried treasure map. I mean, it could help you find your uncle."

She dangled the words *buried treasure map* like fishing bait—and Asher swallowed them, hook, line, and sinker. He swung his head toward Mason so quickly, he nearly lost his helmet. "She's got a map!" he said. "If we go with her to find the treasure, maybe we can find Uncle Bart, too!"

Or maybe we can find some food, thought Mason. *Or a place to sleep that isn't filled with deadly mobs.*

When Luna gestured again toward the waves, Mason hesitated. Then he thought of the suspicious stew. *Sometimes when you take a risk, good things happen.* That's what Asher had said.

Following Luna into the water was a risk. But staying here onshore, with no food or shelter, was a risk, too.

So Mason finally nodded. He took a tiny step forward, like a baby turtle heading toward the sea.

CHAPTER 4

Mason followed Asher's trail of bubbles, keeping an eye on his brother as they swam into deeper water. Asher was a better swimmer underwater than he was at the surface. But compared to Luna's long, strong strokes, Asher's arms hacked at the water, and he barely kicked at all.

Mason took his eyes off his brother for just a second and looked down. *Whoa!*

Rainbow-colored coral seemed to stretch out to eternity. Clusters of pink, purple, and yellow coral dotted the sandy reef. Tall fire-red "trees" of coral stretched up from the ocean floor, surrounded by sprouts of sea grass. And tropical fish darted in, out, and all around the vibrant reef. Mason veered left to avoid swimming through a school of neon green fish with bright blue eyes.

He held his breath until his lungs burned. Then he remembered he didn't *have* to. He was wearing a turtle helmet! Luna said that it would help him breathe underwater, at least for a little while. Mason wondered how long a "little while" would be. Long enough to get all the way down to Luna's underwater home?

He took in a deep inhale of saltwater, which cooled his lungs. Then he swam past Asher and waved his arm, urging Asher to swim faster—before the effect of their helmets wore off.

Luna was swimming upward now, straight to the surface. Had she run out of air?

Mason noticed for the first time that Luna wasn't wearing a helmet. She hadn't been wearing one yesterday, either, when she had first shown up at the beach. But she swam like a turtle in the water—slowly and gracefully, as if she had all the time in the world.

As soon as they broke through the surface, Mason took a deep gulp of *real* air and then searched for Asher. Where was he?

His brother's red head finally popped up. After Asher blew the water from his nose, he began doggy paddling. "Why . . . are . . . we stopping?" he asked, struggling to stay upright.

Luna pointed to a mass of swirling water a few yards away. "We're taking the bubble column down," she said. "It's like a whirlpool. It's the quickest way."

A whirlpool? As Mason studied the churning water, his stomach churned, too. He remembered a whirlpool like this one. The cyclone of water had nearly destroyed their ship! He remembered the power of the waves sucking them downward.

"No way," he said quickly. "We're not swimming anywhere near that whirlpool."

Luna stared at him. "Why not? It'll help you breathe! Once you're inside the bubble column, you won't need your helmet."

Mason shook his head. "I'm good with my helmet, thanks." He reached up to pat the trusty turtle shell.

Luna blew out a breath of impatience. "Your helmet won't work for much longer. It won't get you all the way down to my house, that's for sure."

Mason nervously licked his lips, tasting salt. "Then we'll swim back to the ship," he said. He glanced over his shoulder to see how far they'd come. *Yikes!* Their ship looked like a tiny piece of driftwood washed ashore. They'd never be able to make it back that far—not without a boat!

A splash of water from Asher reminded Mason that his brother couldn't doggy paddle for much longer. And there wasn't another boat in sight.

"We should never have come . . . " he started to say. But what good would it do to scold Luna now, or himself? *Stay calm,* thought Mason. *Figure it out.*

After another deep breath, he knew there was only one choice. They had to follow Luna. If that bubble column was the only way to safety, they'd have to take it. "Show us," he said. "Lead the way."

Luna grinned and then dove underwater, quick as a dolphin. Asher and Mason could barely keep up as she swam toward a column of spiraling bubbles. When they reached it, Mason grabbed Asher's arm.

They swam into the column of bubbles together—and instantly zoomed straight down. Mason lost his stomach as the watery world sped by. Down, down, down they sank, until Luna pulled them out of the bubbles and onto the ocean floor.

There, Mason saw another column of bubbles—this one heading up, like an elevator. Asher stepped toward it, as if he wanted to try out that one, too.

But Luna was already swimming away. She swam toward what looked like an underwater village. *C'mon!* she urged with a backward glance and the wave of her hand.

The village spread out before them like an underwater temple: crumbly stone buildings, huts made of sandstone, and staircases that stretched upward, leading to nowhere. Mason could see it all so clearly, and then he realized why. The village was lit by sea lanterns!

The turquoise-colored blocks cast a soft, warm glow. Luna swam between them, as if they lit her pathway home. Mason reached out to touch a lantern. Would it be hot? No. The prismarine felt smooth and cool beneath his fingers.

But when he looked up again, Luna had disappeared. He opened his mouth to call for her, forgetting that they were underwater. Her name came out in a gurgle of bubbles, which rose upward and then were gone.

Mason swam toward where he had last seen Luna—over a ridge of stone and down the other side. Here the stones were dark as obsidian. But Luna was nowhere to be found.

Panic rose in Mason's chest. What if they lost Luna? How would they find their way back to shore before they ran out of air?

As he turned to swim back, a black stone shifted. Two white eyes blinked, gazing warily at Mason. Thick black sea grass swirled around the stone. *Wait, no— not sea grass*, thought Mason, searching for the word. *Tentacles!* Eight tentacles sprouted from the stone.

Then the squid spun sideways, revealing a gaping red mouth with sharp teeth. It released a cloud of black ink.

And suddenly, Mason couldn't see a thing.

CHAPTER 5

Mason yelped and tried to swim away. But in the murky black water, he didn't know which way was "away"—or even which way was up!

He spun around, felt his way across the rocky ledge with his hands, and kicked his legs as hard as he could. Another kick sent him forward through swirls of inky water. And with one last kick, the water cleared.

Someone hovered in the water above him: Luna. Her face scrunched into a scowl, as if he had done something wrong. But what? She whirled around and led him toward another rocky ledge.

Asher floated near the rocks. Luna swam straight past him and *through* the ledge. With one kick, she disappeared. And Asher followed.

"Wait!" Mason wanted to cry. But it was too late. Asher was gone.

With a few panicked strokes, Mason reached the rocks. He patted the rocks with his hand, searching for a hole in the ledge—and instantly found it. Were there more squid inside? Or . . . something worse?

Asher went in, Mason reminded himself. *So I have to go, too.* He used his arms to pull himself downward and propel his body through the tunnel.

The space was so tight! Mason held his breath, afraid he might get stuck. Only the glowing light at the end of the tunnel—and the thought of finding Asher there—kept him moving forward.

When he popped out into a lantern-lit room, he was shocked to see Luna and Asher floating beside a regular wooden door. What was it doing at the bottom of the sea?

Luna opened the door and swam through it, pulling Asher with her. As soon as Mason had passed through, too, Luna pushed the door shut. Then Mason saw another door.

When he reached to open it, Luna held up her hand. She pointed downward. They were standing on a squishy yellow mat—a porous sponge block. And as Mason watched in wonder, the sponge began to soak up the water that filled the tiny room. Lower and lower the water sank, until Mason's head popped out the top, and then Asher's and Luna's. Mason shivered in his wet clothes—his wet *ink*-covered clothes.

"What happened?" asked Asher, touching the black streak on the front of Mason's blue T-shirt.

"A squid happened, that's what," said Luna. Her brow furrowed again. "Why'd you go and scare my buddy Edward like that?"

"Edward?" cried Mason. "Who names a squid? And anyway, I didn't scare him. *He* scared *me!*"

Luna fought back a smile. "You're scared of squid? That poor thing wouldn't hurt a turtle."

Mason felt heat rise to his cheeks. "Well, it sure knows how to ruin a shirt." He rubbed at the stain, but finally gave up.

When the sponge beneath their feet was bloated with water, Luna opened the second door, revealing a large light-filled room. The walls were made of glass. As a school of brightly colored fish passed by, Mason felt the urge to hold his breath again. But this house—this underwater room of glass—was air-tight.

"Wow," said Asher, hurrying into the room. "Cool. Are your parents home?"

Mason glanced toward the hallway across the room, half expecting Luna's mom or dad to appear right now and greet them. *And maybe offer us a snack,* he thought as his stomach twisted.

But Luna shook her head. "My parents are . . . gone."

"Gone where?" asked Asher. "Are they coming back soon?" He fired off questions like a dispenser shoots off fireballs.

Luna narrowed her eyes, as if she were about to scold Asher for being so nosy. Instead, she said, "C'mon, let's go dry off near the furnace." She reached for the wet sponge mat in the entryway, too, a stream of water dripping behind her as she carried the mat across the room.

What's up? thought Mason. *Why does this girl get weird when Asher asks about her parents?*

As she led them down the long stone hall, Mason followed. The furnace room at the end felt toasty and warm. While Luna dried out the sponge in the furnace, Mason stood beside it, warming his hands.

"Can we see your buried treasure map now?" Asher blurted.

"What's the rush?" asked Luna. "You just got here!"

Asher sighed and threw up his hands. "What do you mean, what's the rush? You said your map could help us find Uncle Bart, didn't you?"

Mason watched Luna's face, wondering if she'd been telling the truth. If she really did have a buried treasure map, why wasn't she eager to bust the thing out and find that treasure?

When Luna stayed silent, Asher talked faster—and louder. "Or maybe your map will help us find the Heart of the Sea. We can give it to Uncle Bart when he comes back. Then we can help him craft a conduit with the Heart of the Sea and nautilus shells!" Asher's eyes drifted upward, as if he were crafting the conduit right now in his mind.

Luna's face brightened. "Nautilus shells? I can help you find some of those."

She rummaged through what looked like a supply chest next to the furnace. Mason expected her to come back out with an armful of shells. Instead, she handed Asher a fishing pole, glowing purple with some sort of enchantment.

Asher's eyes glowed, too. "Luck of the sea?" he asked.

She grinned and nodded. "You'll catch more treasures than fish with this enchanted pole. Maybe even some nautilus shells. But we'll have to go back outside, so grab your helmet."

The thought of going back into the water made Mason shiver from head to toe. Luna must have noticed. "You can stay in and smelt some kelp for dinner," she told him.

Smelt some kelp for dinner. Those were five words that Mason had never heard before, and they didn't exactly make him drool with hunger. But Luna showed him how to put fresh kelp in the furnace. It came out crispy and salty, like thin slices of roasted potato.

Mason placed a piece on his tongue and closed his eyes as it melted away. *Yum!* He loaded more into the furnace, and then tried not to eat every last bite of what he had already taken out.

He glanced around the furnace room, hoping for a distraction. Luna's supply chest sat in the corner. *Is her buried treasure map in there?* he wondered.

It wouldn't be right to snoop—unless he went in there to get something he actually needed. He thought fast. Maybe there were some potatoes in that chest to go with the dried kelp. *Yeah, that'd be a good reason to open someone else's trunk,* he decided.

But as he lifted the dusty lid, he didn't see any potatoes. Just more turtle shells, lots of leather armor, a pickaxe, and a spear with three sharp prongs on the end. *A trident,* he remembered Uncle Bart calling the one on his own cabin wall. For some reason, the weapon sent a trickle of nervousness down Mason's spine. Uncle Bart had used his only for his most dangerous enemies, like the drowned.

Remembering his dream about being attacked by the drowned, Mason dropped the chest lid with a *bang*—and then heard wet, squishy footsteps coming down the hall.

As Asher stepped into the furnace room, he proudly handed over a spiral-shaped nautilus shell. "We got one!" he announced. "We only need like seven more to build that conduit."

Luna carried a bucket full of tropical fish. "To go with the dried kelp," she said. "Plum blockfish, sky-orange snooper, and orange-lime dashers. Yum!"

"Wait, we eat those?" said Asher, pointing at the colorful fish.

She nodded.

He wrinkled his nose. "You're probably going to say that when you cook 'em, they taste like chicken, right?"

She laughed. "Ah, no. We don't cook tropical fish. We eat them raw."

Asher blew out his cheeks and backed out of the room, putting some distance between himself and those raw fish.

"What's his problem?" asked Luna. "You'd think I was trying to get him to eat pufferfish or something."

Mason shrugged. "Picky eater. The poor kid is

probably going to starve to death down here." He was only half-joking.

Then they heard Asher holler from down the hall. "Hey, is this your treasure chest?"

Mason saw panic spread across Luna's face like wildfire. "Don't open that!" she hollered, racing out of the room.

The treasure chest sat against the wall of a crafting room. By the time Mason got there, Asher had his hand on the lid and Luna had practically teleported to his side. "*Don't* open it," she said again.

Her tone was so sharp that Asher actually obeyed. Mason watched his brother's hand slide off the trunk and down to his side. "But isn't your buried treasure map in there?" Asher asked.

Luna hesitated. "I'll get it myself," she said. "Give me some space." As she lifted the lid of the trunk an inch or two, she waved Asher backward.

What's she hiding in there? Mason wondered. *Diamonds? Emeralds? The Heart of the Sea?* Whatever it was, she didn't want to share it. She slid a folded map out of the chest and slammed the lid tight.

As she opened the map on the floor and smoothed out the creases, Asher squatted beside her. "Yes!" he said. "This is the same one Uncle Bart had. That's good, right?" He looked up at Mason. "If we find the treasure, maybe we'll find him, too!"

Mason studied the map. It did look like Uncle Bart's, with creases in all the same places. He pictured his uncle's face printed on the map, right next to the big red X. Would they find Uncle Bart near the buried treasure?

No, Asher's plan made no sense! If Uncle Bart had found the treasure, why wouldn't he have come back to them by now? *Because he can't,* thought Mason. *He's gone. Mystery solved.*

So while Asher babbled on about finding Uncle Bart and his hidden treasure, Mason made a plan of a different kind—figuring out what Luna was hiding. If she had the map, why hadn't she gone after the buried treasure herself? And what else was hidden in that treasure chest?

Most of all, Mason wondered, could she be trusted? Because right now, he and his brother were trapped underwater with no food, weapons, or armor of their own—and no plan for how to get back to dry land.

Right now, this secretive girl was the only hope of survival they had.

CHAPTER 6

"**W**hy can't we go *now*?" Asher whined to Luna. "We have the buried treasure map, so what are we waiting for?"

Mason expected Luna to come up with another excuse or to pull something else out of her supply chest to distract Asher. But she didn't. Instead, she stoked the furnace. Then she sat back down and studied the map. "It looks like we'll have to swim past an ocean monument." She pointed.

Ocean monument? Mason peered over her shoulder, hoping to catch a glimpse of a giant underwater pyramid. But the map looked mostly blank. There was a red X at the top, marking the treasure, and a white dot at the bottom, showing where Luna and the boys were now. "Where's the monument?" Mason asked.

"I don't know for sure," said Luna, "but I think that's what this is." She used her finger to trace a scrawled shape in the lower half of the map. "We'll know more as soon as we start to swim. But it's a long ways away." She glanced at Asher with concern.

She doesn't think he can make it that far! realized Mason. Now he was worried, too.

"Wait," said Asher, his eyes flashing. "Why would we swim *past* a monument? Uncle Bart says there's gold inside those things!"

Luna rolled her eyes. "So you're saying you want to stop and look for gold on the way to finding buried treasure?"

He grinned and nodded.

Just like Uncle Bart, Mason thought again.

"Well gold isn't the only thing in an ocean monument," cautioned Luna. "There are guardians protecting it. They're like huge pufferfish that'll shoot lasers at you the second they see you. And elder guardians that'll give you miner's fatigue and make it almost impossible to escape. So, no, we're not stopping. We're swimming right on by."

Asher heaved an exaggerated sigh. He looked to Mason for help, but Mason only shrugged.

"She said they're like pufferfish," he reminded Asher. "You *hate* pufferfish."

"Yeah," Asher admitted, but his eyes got that faraway look, which meant he hadn't given up on that gold.

"Stay here," said Luna as she left the room. Soon the boys heard the creak of the treasure chest lid in the crafting room next door. When Luna came back, she carefully balanced three glass bottles in her hands.

"Potions?" asked Asher.

She nodded. "Water breathing, swiftness, and night vision. We'll drink these before we go."

Before we go. So Luna was agreeing to lead them on a hunt for buried treasure. Mason's stomach flip-flopped like a fish in a bucket, especially when Luna reached into her supply chest for her sharp trident.

"Do you want a weapon, too?" She glanced at Mason.

His mouth went dry, but he knew the right answer. "Sure." Whatever they ran into on their journey for buried treasure, he had to be ready. When Luna handed him a dusty iron sword from behind the furnace, he took it.

"How about me?" asked Asher.

She shook her head. "I'm fresh out. Besides, you'll need both hands for swimming. I've got some armor you can wear though, and a pickaxe for your pack."

Asher scowled, but he didn't argue when she handed him a worn leather chestplate and a pickaxe.

She handed a chestplate to Mason, too, and gave both boys backpacks—"in case we actually find that treasure," she said with a grin.

When it was time to leave the safety of the under-water home, she pulled out her potions. "This one first," she said, shaking up a bottle of light blue liquid. She uncorked the bottle and handed it to Asher. "You like carrots, right?"

Mason held his breath. Sure, Asher would eat roasted carrots in a pinch. But they weren't exactly his favorite food. So he was shocked when Asher took a quick swig. "Not bad," he said, wiping his mouth.

Mason took a drink of the potion of night vision, too. And it really did taste like carrots.

Then Luna handed Asher another bottle. "Potion of swiftness is sweet," she said. "Made with sugar."

Sugar? She'd said the magic word. Asher practically grabbed that bottle out of her hands, and when he went back for another swig, Mason had to cut him off.

"Save some for the rest of us," he joked. But he savored his own long sip of the sweet potion, trying to remember the last time he and Asher had eaten or drank anything that tasted so good.

When Luna handed Asher the last bottle, he uncorked it and took a huge gulp—then practically spit it out.

"Swallow it! Quick!" said Luna. "Potion of water breathing. You're going to need it. It'll help you breathe underwater longer than your turtle shell helmets will."

Asher forced himself to swallow, but his whole body shuddered. "Ew!!!" he cried as a trickle of potion ran down his chin.

"Sorry," she said with a shrug. "That one's made with pufferfish."

Mason held his nose as he took his own drink. Asher was right—potion of water breathing was disgusting. But as Mason glanced through the glass window, the potion of night vision he had swallowed kicked in. The world outside the glass was suddenly crystal clear. Mason could see every nook and cranny in the sandstone, every stalk of sea grass, and the tiny ridges on the fins of the tropical fish that swam past. "Look!" he cried to Asher.

The view seemed to help Asher forget about the fish-flavored drink he'd just taken. "Let's get out there!" he cried.

Luna nodded. "That's the spirit. C'mon!" She slid the potion bottles into her backpack along with the buried treasure map. Then she reached for her trident and led the boys toward the entryway.

Mason tightened his turtle helmet and grabbed his weapon, hoping he wouldn't need it. He crossed the room in what felt like three quick steps. The potion of swiftness was kicking in, too, and he suddenly felt invincible. *If there's buried treasure out there,* he decided, *we're going to find it!*

* * *

Whoa. As Mason swam around a rocky pillar, the view stretched out before him. The underwater ruins of Luna's village had been cool, but they were nothing compared to the ocean monument.

The sprawling pyramid of prismarine rose toward the water's surface, over twenty blocks tall. Pillars propped up the base of the monument, and sea lanterns lit a long narrow entryway.

Mason glanced over his shoulder to be sure his brother was swimming around the monument instead of *toward* it. Asher was there, close behind, but he craned his neck, staring at the monument in wonder.

Luna waved them onward—a reminder that the potions they'd drunk wouldn't last forever. But a shadow blocked her path.

Mason sucked in his breath and looked up. A squid hovered near the top of a pillar, like a cocoa bean dangling from a jungle tree. Its tentacles rose and fell with the ocean's currents. Luna swam beneath it without so much as a glance, as if she passed squid every day.

She does, Mason reminded himself. *She even has a pet squid named Edward.* But as Mason swam beneath the critter, he kept an eye on those sticky tentacles, imagining one darting down and wrapping around his body.

With one swift kick, he shot past the squid—thanks to the potion of swiftness. Then he flipped around to make sure his brother was coming, too.

But where was Asher? The water surrounding the prismarine temple was clear blue, vast, and empty, except for spurts of sea grass sprouting here and there like potted plants.

Fear wrapped itself around Mason's heart like an icy tentacle. If Asher had gone inside, searching for gold, he might have come face to face with hostile spiky-tailed guardians. *And Asher doesn't even have a weapon!* Mason remembered.

Quick as a flash, he swam back past the squid. Past the pillars. Around the corner toward the entrance to the monument.

But seconds before he reached it, he already knew what he would find—or *wouldn't* find.

Sure enough, Asher was gone.

CHAPTER 7

Mason hesitated only long enough to wave to Luna, who had circled back to look for him.

Then he shot through a row of pillars at the base of the monument. As he swam into the entry room, he scanned all four corners of the room. Any other day, he might have stopped to examine the walls—prismarine blocks of aqua blue, flecked with dark green and yellow. He might have mined a sea lantern to take home for an underwater base of his own.

But today, his only thought was of Asher. He wished he could call out his brother's name. He strained to hear something from the chambers above, a clue that would help him find his brother in this maze of rooms and tunnels. Then he heard it—the low growl of a hostile mob echoing throughout the monument. Was it the guardian Luna had warned them about?

Swim faster! Mason urged himself forward, through a rectangular room with tall pillars. He sped down a long hallway and through a square room with three more sea lanterns encased in dark prismarine.

The lanterns cast off a soft glow, but a shaft of light from up above caught Mason's eye. He glanced at the ceiling—no, through the ceiling. Someone had tunneled upward to get to a higher chamber. Asher? Mason kicked his legs and darted through the hole.

But Asher wasn't waiting up above. Something else was.

The spiky green fish stared at Mason with its single eye. It hovered for a moment, as if sizing him up. Then it released an eerie growl and lunged, thrashing its barbed tail.

Mason swung his sword. There was no time to think—only time to act. To fight back. To find Asher!

The sword felt slow and heavy underwater. But as it struck the guardian's body, the mob grunted and tumbled sideways. When it righted itself, it glowed red with rage.

Mason saw the laser beam before he felt it—a bluish purple ray that struck his chest. He tried to dodge the ray, to step sideways or duck beneath it. But the beam locked onto his chest and then turned fiery yellow.

The blast that followed knocked Mason backward. He slammed into a pillar. As he slid slowly downward, he fought to catch his breath. He'd been wearing armor, but the blow had still knocked the wind right out of his chest.

When he could finally inhale, he took in a breath of seawater and blew it back out. Then he scurried around the pillar, staying low to the ground—and hoping not to come eye to eye with the guardian.

The hostile mob was swimming forward now, its spikes pulled back into its body. But it seemed to have lost its way. *Is it looking for me?* wondered Mason. *Can't it see me behind this pillar?*

The mob stopped swimming and sank slowly, as if it had lost this game of hide-and-seek. But its eye was watchful.

Mason waited until the guardian had turned away before making a break toward the next room. He tried to swim, kicking his feet furiously, but his body felt heavy as obsidian. He waited for the blast—for a purple ray to light up the chamber and stop him in his tracks.

But the blast never came.

When he finally reached the next room, he blew out a bubbly breath of relief—because there was Asher, treading water, trying to mine his way up through the prismarine ceiling. He swung a pickaxe against the ceiling three times, until a blue-green block tumbled out.

Mason couldn't decide whether to scold his brother or hug him. But as he swam toward him, Asher disappeared through the hole in the ceiling.

Wait! Mason wanted to cry out. Still weak from the blast of the guardian, his limbs felt slow and heavy. *Is the potion of swiftness wearing off?* he wondered.

It couldn't have been—Asher seemed to be swimming at record speed. Mason couldn't catch up with his brother, but he could follow his trail of mined blocks.

They led upward through the monument, level by level.

As Mason pulled his way through another hole in the ceiling, he finally caught sight of Asher. He stood before a sea lantern, his shape silhouetted against the light. Was he going to mine the lantern, too?

As Mason half crawled, half swam toward Asher, a shadow cast over the room. Mason ducked, expecting a guardian to charge him at any moment. But when he found the courage to face the hostile mob, there was nothing there.

As the room dimmed, Mason rubbed his eyes. Then he realized: the potion of night vision was wearing off!

Asher whirled around and raised his pickaxe, as if he thought Mason were a hostile mob.

"It's me!" Mason cried, the words coming out in a stream of bubbles.

Asher lowered his pickaxe, but he rubbed his eyes, too—as if trying to remove the veil of darkness that had fallen over the room.

The potion of night vision had definitely worn off. *Which means another potion will wear off soon,* thought Mason with horror. *The potion of water breathing!*

Asher must have had the same thought, because his green eyes grew wild. So Mason fought down the panic rising in his own chest and tapped his turtle helmet, reminding Asher that their helmets would help with water breathing, too. But only for a little while.

Think fast, thought Mason. *Make a plan.*

They'd never get back to Luna's house—or to the

bubble column—before their turtle helmets stopped working. But could they swim to the water's surface? They'd been working their way up, floor by floor, in the ocean monument. Could they swim the rest of the way?

Search for a window! thought Mason, patting the wall with his hand as if a window would suddenly appear.

He grabbed the pickaxe from Asher's hand and blasted the wall, taking out a block of prismarine with a single blow. His strength was finally returning. But through the hole, he saw only another room. So he struck another wall. And then a third.

He desperately swung his pickaxe. But every room seemed to lead to another—an endless maze of prismarine chambers. It was no use!

As he let the pickaxe float down to his side, he saw a blur of color out of the corner of his eye. Asher was swimming through the hole in the floor. He was heading back, trying to get out the way they'd come in. But there was no time!

Mason dove after him, grasping at his foot. He caught it just in time, and the brothers tumbled through the hole together. Asher kicked, trying to break free. He knocked the turtle helmet right off of Mason's head.

"Stop!" Mason cried, grabbing for his helmet. But as he opened his mouth, water came in.

The saltwater burned his throat.

As Mason began to cough, he let go of Asher's foot.

He spun in a desperate circle, searching for his turtle helmet.

There! In the corner!

Mason lunged for it, swimming for his life. His lungs burned, but he couldn't take a breath—not without the helmet.

His fingers grazed it once. Twice.

And then his world went black.

CHAPTER 8

Mason woke to his brother's face, inches away from his own. Even in the dark, shadowy room, he noticed that Asher's eyes had never looked so green—or so terrified.

Mason jerked upward so quickly, his head began to spin. When he reached up to steady it, he felt the turtle helmet pressed firmly down over his ears. The memory of losing it flooded back, and Mason's heart began to race. *It's okay,* he told himself. *You can breathe now. Take a breath. See?*

The cool water soothed his lungs, but his fear hung around like a cloud of lingering potion. *We're running out of time,* he remembered. *The turtle helmet works for now. But it won't work for long.*

Asher tugged at Mason's hand, leading him back toward the hole in the ground. He still wanted to go down—back the way they'd came. Finally, Mason gave in.

As they swam into the lower chamber, Mason spotted a shadowy shape behind a pillar. What was it?

Without potion of night vision, he could barely see his hand in front of his face. He reached for the sword at his side.

But as the shape swam out from behind the pillar, Mason recognized Luna. Asher swam quickly to her side and reached for her pack, but she was already unzipping it. When she pulled out a bottle of potion, Mason was hit with realization, as if a sea lantern had just gone on in his mind. Asher wasn't trying to swim out of the monument. He was trying to get back to Luna—to get more potions!

Asher guzzled them down one by one—flinching only a little when he drank the fishy, foul-tasting potion of water breathing. Then Luna offered the bottles to Mason. He drank greedily, eager for the shadows in the room to disappear—for the warm glow of potion of night vision to return. When it came, he relaxed, breathing deeply.

Luna drank her share of the potions, too. Then she waved them toward the hole in the floor. It was time to go back—and this time, Mason was ready to follow.

But as Luna lowered herself into the hole, she froze . . . and then swam back out. She touched her finger to her lips, warning the boys not to make a sound. Mason crept to the hole to take a look.

A hulking green guardian lurked in the water below, and the mob was not alone. Mason could see the spiky tail of another guardian. And was that a third that just swam by? He glanced up at Luna. *Now what?*

She hesitated for a moment, studying the passage-way into the next room. Then she shrugged as if to say, *What choice do we have?* Together, side by side, Mason and Luna swam toward the doorway, with Asher close behind.

When they were safely inside the next room, Luna stopped and pulled her map from her backpack. She opened it up and slid her finger just below the heavy crease of a fold line. Mason thought again of Uncle Bart's map—of the many hours his uncle had spent unfolding the map, studying it, and folding it back up again. His heart squeezed, remembering his uncle's face. But he shook off the memory. Luna needed his help finding a way out of this monument. So Mason reached out to hold the map, which kept trying to float away.

The lower half of the map had filled in now, and Mason could clearly see the ocean monument. It was square-shaped, with the entrance in the lower front and two long winged structures on either side. A white dot showed that the kids were near the center of the mon-ument—nowhere near the entrance.

Not even close, thought Mason. How had they come so far in such a short time?

Luna slid her finger upward, through the back side of the monument toward the red X at the top. She glanced at Mason as if to say, *Should we go this way?*

There wasn't another entrance. So did Luna think they could mine their way out?

Asher waved the pickaxe at his side—he was up for the challenge. Luna stared at him hard for a moment.

Mason could almost read her thoughts. *Why should we let you tunnel us out? You're the one who got us into this mess!*

When Luna finally gave Asher a thumbs-up, Mason breathed a sigh of relief. They had a plan B—B for "busting our way out of here." And it was time to go, before guardians began spawning in this room, too.

Luna led the way with her map, swimming through doorways when she could find them. And when she couldn't, Asher mined through prismarine blocks and bricks with his pickaxe. Mason stayed far enough away to avoid the swing of the pickaxe but close enough that he could be at his brother's side if he ran smack into a hostile mob.

As they swam down a long hallway and around a corner, Asher suddenly stopped. Mason bumped into his backside so hard, he had to reach out for the wall to steady himself.

Asher hovered in a doorway, frozen like a prismarine statue. What had he found? Blocks of gold? Or . . . guardians?

As Mason gazed over his brother's shoulder, he saw it, too. In the middle of the tall chamber stood a wall of dark prismarine. The blocks were arranged in a giant plus sign, with a sea lantern tucked in each corner.

Asher turned toward Luna with a questioning look.

When she caught up and saw the dark prismarine blocks, her eyes widened. She grabbed Asher's pickaxe, but he wouldn't let go. So she tugged him toward the prismarine and pointed, as if to say, *Mine it! C'mon, hurry!*

But what did Luna want with those blocks? Mason wondered.

Asher seemed confused, too, but after he took his first whack at the dark prismarine, he pumped his fist in the air.

What? wondered Mason. He swam closer. Then he saw the brilliant sheen of the treasure beneath the prismarine. *Gold.* They'd found the gold Uncle Bart had told them about!

One shiny block fell to the chamber floor with a *thud,* which echoed throughout the watery room. As Asher struggled to lift it, Mason met Luna's eyes. Was she thinking what he was thinking? *We'll never be able to get that home!* he suddenly realized.

Asher must have figured it out, too. Instead of mining the next block of gold, he used his pickaxe to break the first block into a pile of gold ingots. Then he began scooping them into his backpack. He waved at Mason and Luna to help him.

The bars of gold felt smooth and surprisingly heavy. Mason fit three into his pack and then zipped it shut. He hoisted the bag onto his shoulders. Even underwater, he could feel the weight of that gold.

When Asher looked back longingly at all the gold they were leaving behind, Mason tugged on his hand. *C'mon, brother,* he wanted to say. *For once, just let it go.*

Finally, Asher did. But the look on his face told Mason that one day, he'd be back for that gold.

Just like Uncle Bart, thought Mason. *Always searching for treasure.*

As they swam down a long corridor, Mason stopped to adjust his pack. He barely noticed when Luna stopped swimming. Or when Asher turned to wave at him wildly.

Mason looked up, just in time to hear the low growl of a hostile mob. *Guardian!*

Luna whirled around, as if heading back the way they had just come. But the look on her face told Mason all he needed to know. There were more guardians behind him.

They were surrounded.

CHAPTER 9

As a fluorescent purple laser lit up the hall, Mason sprang into action. He slid his sword from his side and spun in a circle, deciding which mob to attack first. Then he remembered—Asher didn't have a weapon!

Except Asher seemed to think he did.

Mason turned just in time to see Asher charge a guardian with his pickaxe. The spiky green mob growled and then fired off another laser, straight at Asher.

No! Mason swam past his brother—darting in front of him to block the laser before it was fully charged. When the laser turned yellow, he squeezed his eyes shut and braced himself for the blast, ready to take damage.

But nothing happened. When he heard a grunt, he opened his eyes. Luna's trident was stuck in the guardian's side! It screeched and rolled sideways, thrashing its tail side to side, trying to ditch the weapon.

Another purple laser hit the prismarine wall,

reminding Mason that there were more mobs to fight. Asher was already swimming toward the mob at the other end of the hall. Mason tried to catch up, fumbling to swim with the sword in his hand.

Stop! he wanted to call to Asher. *Don't try to fight it without me!*

But Asher couldn't catch the guardian. The fishlike mob was swimming *away* from him. Why?

Mason got his answer a moment later, when the mob fired off another laser. It had taken a few seconds to recharge, but now it was back with a fury. The beam bounced off a prismarine pillar, missing Asher's head by mere inches.

"Now!" Mason cried, his word getting lost in a flurry of bubbles. *Attack the guardian now, before it can recharge!*

He reached the mob in seconds and struck it with his sword. Asher was there, too, swinging his pickaxe. Again and again they struck the beast, until they saw the blood-red glow of its defeat. The mob sunk to the chamber floor.

Asher instantly dove to collect the guardian drops—a couple of prismarine shards.

No! Mason lunged to grab his brother's arm. *There's no time!* Luna needed their help fighting the other guardian. So Mason tugged Asher away from the treasure and back toward Luna.

When they reached her side, Mason raised his sword, but she held out her hand to stop him. *Wait!* she seemed to be saying. But for what?

The guardian waited, too, its thorny orange spikes raised and ready for battle. A second later, it charged. As it swam toward them, those spikes disappeared. And that's when Luna struck, using her trident like a sword.

Mason and Asher fought, too. When Asher hit the mob's tail with his pickaxe, it turned in retreat. Luna took aim with her trident and sent the weapon spiraling through the water.

It struck the mob dead center. With an angry growl, the guardian rolled sideways and began to sink. Then it was gone.

So was Asher, diving toward the drops to collect his latest treasure.

Mason swam toward a pillar instead, taking a moment to catch his breath. They'd done it. They'd fought off the guardians—together!

As Luna retrieved her trident, Mason swam down to his brother's side. Asher held out a prismarine shard. Then he pointed to another drop—something yellowish lodged beneath a loose stone.

Was it a golden apple? Mason squinted to make out the drop. But as soon as Asher touched it, he pulled his hand away. Then he kicked at it with disgust.

Mason swam closer, curious to know what kind of drop Asher would reject. Then he saw the tiny spikes on the small yellow ball. It wasn't a golden apple at all. It was a pufferfish! *Ha!*

Luna had gathered some drops of her own—two raw cod fish. When she offered one to Asher, he blew out his cheeks, looking like he might lose his lunch. He shook his head and swam away.

Mason watched his brother speed around a corner. He wanted to remind him to keep his pickaxe out—that there might be more guardians ahead.

But it was too late.

As Asher's feet gave one last kick and disappeared, Mason heard the growl of the guardian—and saw a blast of light.

Mason sped down the hall. He rounded the corner just in time to see the guardian's laser turn yellow. Just in time to see Asher knocked backward into the wall. Just in time to spot the beast that had fired the laser.

This guardian was enormous, twice the size of the others. Its scales were grey, not green, with sharp purple spikes. It was an elder guardian—Mason knew it for sure now. And its single eye was trained on Asher.

Mason dove toward his brother. He floated hunched over, with his arms hugging his body. Mason tried to lift him, but he felt like dead weight. *His back-pack is full of gold,* Mason remembered. So he swam beneath his brother, propping Asher up on his back like a turtle shell.

But how could Mason fight? He could barely reach for his sword, let alone use it! As the elder guardian flicked its thorny tail, Mason half-swam, half-crept toward a prismarine pillar—a wall of safety.

But the growl of the guardian rang off the walls. The mob was still watching. This mob wouldn't let him go.

Mason prepared for the blast—for the laser that would destroy him.

Take your best shot, thought Mason, squeezing his eyes shut. *You can hit me, beast. But not my brother.*

And then the room lit up with light.

CHAPTER 10

The laser hit the wall inches from Mason's face. He sucked in a wave of water and blew it back out, trying not to panic. Was the elder guardian recharging, preparing to blast them again? Or was he swimming toward them now?

Mason couldn't bring himself to look around the side of the pillar. Instead, he hoisted Asher higher on his back and reached for his sword. If the elder guardian charged, Mason would have to fight. There was no other choice.

Then he heard a grunt. Something or someone had struck the hostile mob. Luna! She had arrived with her trident—just in time.

The blast sent the guardian spinning. But as it righted itself, it let loose an eerie growl. Mason felt the wave of water, the pressure building as the mob charged. And then it was right in front of him.

Mason plunged his sword into the beast's belly and pushed off from it, sliding along the wall away from

65

the mob. Asher stirred and struggled to break free from Mason's grip, but Mason wouldn't let his brother go. *Not till we're safe,* he told himself. *Not till we get away.*

They crept along the wall until it gave way to an opening. Then Mason turned and swam, hovering along the floor under the weight of his brother. A blast of light told him that Luna was still fighting.

And she had to win. *She has to!* thought Mason. How would they get out of this monument and back to safety without her? Without her potions?

As Asher kicked his feet, trying to break free, Mason finally let him go. But as soon as Asher tried to swim, he sunk to the prismarine floor. The guardian's laser had gotten him good. Had it missed his chestplate? Or blasted right through?

Another grunt sounded from the room next door, followed by silence. Mason held his breath as he watched the doorway, waiting for the second when they would see Luna's victorious face—or the hostile eye of the elder guardian.

When Luna came into view, Mason blew out a bubbly breath. *Yes!* But there was no time to celebrate. As soon as Luna saw Asher floating weakly near the floor, she flung her backpack off her shoulder and reached inside.

Mason expected her to pull out a potion of some sort—something that would cure Asher. Instead, she pulled out her map. She gave it a quick check, slid it back into her backpack, and then darted toward Asher and grabbed his pickaxe.

She pointed toward the back wall as if to say, *This way. This is our way out the back of the monument.* She swung the pickaxe at a prismarine brick halfway down the wall.

And nothing happened.

Luna swung again, this time at a regular block of prismarine.

Still nothing.

When Mason reached for the pickaxe, she hung on for a moment—but she finally let go. He swung the pickaxe with all his strength at the wall. The force sent a wave of pain through his shoulder, but the block didn't so much as crack.

What had Luna said about the elder guardians? Mason struggled to remember. *They'll give you miner's fatigue and make it impossible to escape.* Is that what was happening now? Miner's fatigue?

Mason swung the pickaxe at a sea lantern and then at the floor, trying to break anything. But his arms were exhausted and sore. He set down the pickaxe in defeat.

That's when Luna disappeared. She swam away—flew off like a trident. Mason watched her dart through a doorway without so much as a goodbye or a wave of her hand.

How was he supposed to follow? Asher was too weak—and too heavy to carry. Luna knew that! So where had she gone? Had she decided to save herself and leave them to . . . die?

Rage bubbled inside Mason's chest. He'd known from the start that there was something he couldn't trust about Luna. *We never should have followed her,* he thought again. *I never should have let Asher talk me into that!*

The room suddenly grew dark, as if someone had switched off a torch. That could only mean one thing—Mason's potion of night vision was wearing off again. And Luna was nowhere to be found.

Mason felt a stab of ice-cold fear. Would potion of water breathing wear off next?

He darted from one side of the room to the other, as if pacing underwater. Faster and faster, like a mob spinning in a red-hot spawner. He wanted to blast out of the walls of the monument. Swim to the water's surface with his brother. Find their way back to Uncle Bart's boat.

But it was all so far away.

We're doomed, thought Mason. He fell into a floating heap of hopelessness beside Asher.

That's when Luna came back.

Mason shot upward and pointed at her backpack. "We need potions!" he tried to say.

But Luna wasn't listening. She waved at him furiously, swimming just a short ways into the room and then back out, like a wolf that wanted to be followed. *C'mon!* her eyes hollered. *Follow me!*

Mason tugged on Asher, swimming with him out from the room. Luna led them down a short corridor, through a long, narrow room, and then . . . into the strangest room Mason had ever seen. He stopped swimming and hugged the doorframe for support.

The ceiling of the room was covered with giant yellow sponges. The wet, bloated blocks swayed side to side, threatening to drop any second with an enormous *splat*.

Luna swam into the room, beneath a low-hanging sponge. As Mason followed, pulling Asher carefully behind, he saw that the center of the room had been tunneled out. Was Luna going to lead them down the tunnel toward an exit?

No—instead, she swam *up*, past the hanging sponges toward the ceiling. When Mason popped his head out of the water beside her, he realized why. She had found a pocket of air!

He quickly pulled up his brother beside him. Asher blinked twice and wiped his weary face with his hands. "What happened? Did we get out?"

Luna wrung out her ponytail. "We can't get out—not until the miner's fatigue wears off. But we can rest here. The sponges soak up some of the water."

Her voice sounded so strange, now that it wasn't passing through gallons of water before reaching Mason's ears. He tried out his own voice, too, coughing out a mouthful of saltwater before inhaling dry, cool air. "Should we drink more potion?" he asked. The room was so dim, even the bright yellow sponges seemed dark and dingy.

Luna shook her head. "We need to save it for the swim back home."

Asher's ears pricked at her words. "Home? No! We're searching for buried treasure!"

"You're the one who took a detour!" Mason reminded him. "And you already have a backpack full of gold. Plus, you're weak from a fight with an elder guardian. So Luna's right. We're going back." *If we ever get out of this place,* he thought with a shiver.

Luna pulled out her map to show Asher. "See how far away we still are from the treasure?" she said. "We'll go after it another day. And next time, maybe you'll stick to the plan." She shot him a stern glance.

"I can't see the map," Asher grumbled. "It's too dark."

Luna pulled a sea pickle from her backpack. When she held it underwater, it lit up like a torch. The pickle cast a warm glow on the ceiling of the room, which reflected back onto the map.

The white dot showing where they were now was almost exactly on the centerline of the map. They were *almost* out of the monument—if they could only break through another block or two, they'd be free.

Mason studied the map again, trying to find a way out. But the center of the map was so worn, he couldn't read the map. He thought again of Uncle Bart's map, which was worn in all the same places. Luna must have guarded her map the same way he guarded his, ever since finding it in a shipwreck at the ocean's floor.

"Where did you find your map?" Mason asked. Had Luna found a shipwreck nearby?

She folded the map quickly and shrugged her shoulders. "I don't really remember. I've had it for a while."

"Did you find it on a pirate ship?" asked Asher, taking the words right out of Mason's mouth.

Luna shrugged again and then reached for the pickaxe. She started to tap at the nearest sponge.

But Mason couldn't let it go. How could she *not* remember if she'd found the map in a shipwreck? And if she'd had the map for a while, why hadn't she gone looking for the treasure yet? Why was she acting so mysterious about the map?

Maybe she stole it.

The four words sounded in Mason's mind as clearly as if someone had spoken them. *Maybe it belongs to someone else.*

Maybe . . .

Mason pictured Uncle Bart's face.

Maybe this doesn't just look like Uncle Bart's map. Maybe this is *Uncle Bart's map!*

CHAPTER 11

Mason's stomach squeezed. But before he could confront Luna about the map, the sponge she was mining broke loose from the ceiling. It plunged downward. As it struck the floor, the water below Mason's chin sunk a little lower.

"The pickaxe works!" Luna cried. "Our miner's fatigue is over. Let's get out of here." She dove underwater, but quickly popped back up. "Wait, first things first."

She pulled the potion bottles from her backpack. But all three bottles were nearly empty. Would there be enough to share? And would the potions last long enough to get them back to Luna's house?

Luna's map still niggled at the back of Mason's brain. But he put that worry to rest as he sipped potions of water breathing and night vision, making sure to leave enough for Asher. He gave Asher *all* of his potion of swiftness, since he was still weak from the blast of the elder guardian.

73

When the potions began to kick in, Mason followed Luna through the hole she'd mined into the brightly lit room next door. Over and up, over and up, Luna mined her way through walls and ceilings.

When her pickaxe broke through prismarine and revealed a bright blue sky, Mason nearly shouted with joy. He pushed his way through the hole, half expecting to pop out of the water into the Overworld. But that sky was still a mile away, the sun's light shining down through gallons of water.

They were still submerged in the sea. They were still in danger. With a sigh, Mason helped Asher out of the hole to begin their long journey back to Luna's home.

Asher was stronger now, after resting and drinking the potion of swiftness. But Mason stayed behind with his brother, following Luna. With every stroke she took, he stared at her and wondered: *Who is this girl with so many secrets? Where is her family? Does she have Uncle Bart's map? And does she know what happened to him?*

He promised himself that as soon as they reached her underwater base, he'd find out.

* * *

Yum! Dried kelp had never tasted so good. Mason reached for another bite. He busted Asher licking his salty fingers, too.

They'd been sitting by the furnace for an hour or

so, and their clothes were nearly dry. But Mason wondered if he would ever feel warm again. Every time he thought of the dank, dark ocean monument—the place where he'd feared they might be trapped forever—he shivered.

Luna sat at the table unpacking her backpack. Empty potion bottles. Three gold ingots. A couple of cod fish. And then . . . the folded map.

Mason swallowed hard. He needed to confront her about the map—to find out if it had belonged to Uncle Bart. But he didn't want to ask in front of Asher. *Because maybe Luna didn't actually steal it from Uncle Bart,* Mason realized. *Maybe when she found Uncle Bart, he was already . . . gone.* And the truth about that might crush Asher.

So Mason waited. He listened as Luna returned the potion bottles, gold ingots, and map to the treasure chest down the hall. He watched as Luna carefully cleaned up the cod fish and put them in her supply chest. Then she changed her mind and pulled one back out. "I'm going to go feed this to Edward," she said. "Be right back."

Was this Mason's opportunity to talk to her in private? Maybe. As she left the house, he started to follow her out. But when he passed the room with the treasure chest, where Luna hid something she didn't want the brothers to see, he froze. And turned left. And flung open the lid to the treasure chest before he could talk himself out of it.

The first thing he saw were potion bottles: oodles

of them, filled with liquids in every color of the rainbow. Next to those, Luna had carefully stacked the gold ingots. A few emeralds were scattered throughout the chest. And in the far corner, Luna had spread open the map—as if hiding something underneath.

Mason lifted the corner of the map. When he saw a helmet beneath the map, he blew out a breath of disappointment. The helmet was made of plain old iron—not gold or diamonds. So why did Luna have it in her treasure chest instead of in her regular supply chest?

Then Mason noticed the purple glow. It was an enchanted helmet, probably with respiration. But still . . . what was so special about that? Luna had a bunch of turtle helmets, and she seemed to be able to hold her breath for so long underwater, she rarely even wore them.

Mason checked over his shoulder, worried that Luna might come back in and bust him. As he glanced back down, his eye caught something. The letter *B*. It was engraved in the front of the helmet, a reminder that this helmet belonged to someone—someone Mason knew very well.

This helmet belonged to Uncle Bart.

"Hey! What are you doing?"

As Asher's voice rang out, Mason dropped the lid of the chest. It slammed shut with a *bang*. He whirled around, hoping Luna hadn't heard from outside.

"What are *you* doing?" Mason snapped back. "You shouldn't sneak up on me like that!"

Asher didn't seem the least bit ashamed. He pressed

past Mason toward the chest. "You found something in there. What was it?"

Mason tried to lead him away, but Asher was like a wolf with a bone. *He won't let it go,* Mason realized. *And Luna will be back any minute now.*

So he grabbed Asher's arm and looked him in the eye. "I'll show you, but you can't say anything to Luna, okay? Not yet."

Asher nodded.

Quick as a flash, Mason lifted the lid, slid the map aside, and showed Asher the helmet.

It took a moment for Asher to understand. The disappointment on his face changed to curiosity. And then to excitement. And then . . . to dismay. "Uncle Bart can't be hunting for treasure," Asher whispered. "He can't breathe underwater without his helmet!"

Mason nodded. "I think this is Uncle Bart's map, too." He pointed. "That means Luna knows something about Uncle Bart—about what happened to him. Something she's not telling us."

Asher's forehead furrowed with confusion. "She didn't *hurt* him," he said, as if trying to convince himself. "Luna wouldn't even step on a turtle egg."

"I know," said Mason. "You're right. But she knows something—she has to." As he lowered the lid to the treasure chest, he remembered how she'd defeated the elder guardian with her trident. *She probably didn't hurt Uncle Bart,* thought Mason. *But if she wanted to, she sure could.* Luna was a fierce fighter.

When the front door creaked, Mason warned

Asher again. "Don't say anything. Let me talk to her first, okay?"

There wasn't time to wait for Asher's response. Mason led him down the hall, back to the furnace room, back to the bowl of dried kelp. Mason tried to eat another piece—to act normal, as if the boys had never left their spots at the table in the warm furnace room. But the kelp stuck in his throat.

As Luna came back in, Mason saw Asher's jaw clench. *If I don't say something soon, he will,* Mason realized.

He stood to speak—but Asher beat him to the punch.

"You stole our uncle's helmet!" Asher hollered, sticking his finger right in Luna's face. "And his buried treasure map. Why? Why'd you do that?"

Luna took a giant step backward. "I did *not* steal his map," she shot back. "That's my map. I'm not a thief."

But Asher wouldn't hear a word of it. "Where's Uncle Bart?" he demanded to know.

Luna gave an exasperated sigh. "I don't know!" she cried. "If I did, wouldn't I tell you?"

Her question hung in the air, suspended like lingering potion.

"No," said Mason. The word popped right out of his mouth. "No, you probably wouldn't. You won't tell us what happened to your parents. You won't tell us where you found your map. You were hiding the stuff in that treasure chest. I can't prove you're a thief, but I'm pretty sure you're a liar."

He may as well have struck Luna with a sword. Her eyes looked wounded, but only for a split second. Then she turned on him.

"I'm not lying!" she spat. "I brought you here to help you. I gave you food and tried to help you find your dumb buried treasure. If you think I'm so horrible, you and Asher should just leave. Go. What are you waiting for?" She pointed toward the door.

"Not until you tell us where Uncle Bart is!" said Asher. He crossed his arms.

Mason studied Luna's face. She had shut right down—turned off like a Redstone switch. If she knew what had happened to Uncle Bart, she wasn't going to say. So it was time to go.

Luna disappeared into the furnace room and came back out with two turtle helmets. She tossed one to Asher and practically threw one at Mason. He caught it, but just barely.

"C'mon," he said to Asher, leading him toward the door before Luna threw something worse at them, like a splash potion of harming.

As Mason stepped onto the sponge mat in the entryway, he braced himself for the flood of water that would hit them as soon as they opened the last door.

But what choice did they have? Luna's home wasn't safe anymore. It was time to head back to the ship—or whatever was left of it. He made sure Asher's turtle shell was snug on his head, and then Mason pulled open the door.

The wall of water hit first.

Mason dove forward, eyes closed, keeping a hold of Asher's arm until they could safely close the door behind them. But something was blocking the door. Was Luna tugging on it from the other side?

Mason spun around. It wasn't Luna. And it wasn't a some*one* at all—it was a some*thing*.

A zombie? No, its skin was bluish green, its brown robes tattered. The creature stared at Mason with eerie glowing eyes.

Then the drowned growled and took a step forward, its arms outstretched.

CHAPTER 12

Mason yelped and darted away from the drowned. But, wait . . . *Asher!* He reached back to grab his brother's hand and yank him forward. Then he saw the others.

More drowned were swimming and staggering across the ocean floor—like an army separating the brothers from Luna's home. How many were there? Mason couldn't tell. Darkness was falling, and shadows covered the ocean floor. But nearly a dozen pairs of glowing blue eyes pierced the murky water, all trained on him and his brother.

Asher swam frantically—as fast as he could go. *Will it be fast enough?* Mason worried. He glanced over his shoulder. Two of the drowned were swimming after the boys now, gaining speed with every second.

When Asher turned to him in panic, Mason tried to make a plan. They needed something: A potion of swiftness. Boots enchanted with Depth Strider.

Anything to get them more quickly to the bubble column that would lead them to safety.

But all we have are backpacks loaded down with gold, he realized. *Wait, that's it!*

He released his backpack in seconds, flinging it at the nearest drowned. The heavy pack knocked the drowned backward, slowing him down—at least for a while.

But when Mason tried to tug the pack off Asher's back, his brother fought back, struggling to keep a hold of his treasure.

Forget it! Mason wanted to cry. *Let it go!* But just like Uncle Bart, Asher couldn't. Would he rather die than give up his gold?

Not on my watch, thought Mason. He gave a final tug and yanked the pack off Asher's back. He flung it quickly at the other drowned, before Asher could grab it back. But in his hurry, Mason's aim was off—way off. The backpack tumbled through the water about three feet away from the drowned's mottled head.

As they passed a glowing sea lantern, Mason could see more clearly. This drowned, the one right on their heels, was carrying a *trident*. Mason's heart leaped into his throat.

As they neared the bubble column heading upward, he held his breath, hoping they'd make it in time. He kicked wildly with his feet and slashed through the water with his left arm, tugging Asher forward with his right.

Faster! he willed himself. His heart felt as if it would explode in his chest.

And then they were inside the column.

Mason suddenly felt light as air. The upward current carried him easily—so quickly that he let go of Asher's hand. And for just a moment, he felt safe, as if they might just make it back to the ship. As if everything might be okay.

But as he popped out of the water, he could see the tiny ship bathed in moonlight on the deserted beach. It looked so small, like a toy. And so tattered. And not very safe at all.

When Asher came up, too, spitting water and blowing his nose, Mason put on his bravest face.

This would be a long swim. In the dark. And this time, they wouldn't have Luna by their side.

* * *

Land felt funny beneath Mason's feet. His legs wobbled, as if he hadn't used them for walking in a very long time. The sand slipped beneath his feet, sending him toppling into the shallow waves over and over again.

Asher didn't even try to stand. He swam into shore on his belly, using his hands to pull himself forward until the water ran out altogether. Then he laid his cheek in the sand and rested.

"Not too long now," Mason warned, scanning the beach for mobs. "It's nighttime. We're not safe out here."

"I just need a sec," Asher mumbled. He closed his eyes.

Mason sat beside him, keeping watch. But the tide was rolling in, growing stronger. The night air sent a chill down the back of Mason's wet shirt. And thunder rumbled in the distance.

"C'mon," Mason said, reaching for Asher's hand to help him up. "Storm's coming."

They plodded toward the ship together.

"I feel like Luna attacked me with potion of slowness," Asher whispered.

"Me, too," Mason admitted. She hadn't actually attacked them, but she had pretty much ordered them out of the house. And after lying to them about Uncle Bart's things!

Anger pulsed through Mason's chest like the tide on the moonlit beach. Luna hadn't been a friend after all. *We're on our own again,* he thought. *Just like before.*

Only now, the ship looked more tattered than ever. As they neared the hull, Mason saw charred wood where undead mobs had burned by morning's light. What would the inside of the ship hold?

He hurried forward, willing his legs to move faster. Asher slip-slopped along in the sand behind. It sounded like he was trailing by a mile.

"Hurry up!" Mason called to him. But when he turned around, Asher was right behind him. So who was making the sound near the water?

Mason could barely make out the shape in the shadows. Was it Luna? Had she followed them?

He didn't know whether to be relieved or angry. *I'll wait until I hear what she has to say,* he decided.

But Asher didn't wait. Asher could never wait. He jogged through the sand back toward Luna.

As a flash of lightning lit the sky, the shadowy figure became crystal clear. It wasn't Luna at all.

The drowned held out its arms toward Asher and released a gurgly growl. It took another squishy footstep forward.

And as more shapes emerged from the shallow waves, Mason realized that the drowned wasn't alone.

CHAPTER 13

"**R**un!" Mason cried.

Asher slid to a stop, just feet away from the drowned. He whirled around and started to run. But he moved as if in slow motion—as if after all of that swimming, he just couldn't get his legs to work.

I need a weapon, thought Mason. *Now!* He darted through the hole in the ship's hull, hoping he had left his bow and arrow there. Hoping that it hadn't been destroyed by a mob or stolen by pirates or griefers.

The bow was propped up in the corner, right where Mason had left it the morning Luna had arrived. He grabbed it, ignoring the heaviness in his arms. He placed an arrow in the bow before he had even left the hull. As soon as he stepped back onto the beach, he took aim and fired.

The arrow sailed past Asher, who was struggling to reach the ship. It hit the drowned in the shoulder, knocking it backward. The mob grunted, but he kept coming.

87

Mason loaded another arrow. But now two more drowned had stepped out of the water. He slid his bow side to side, wondering which to strike first. Out of the corner of his eye, he saw Asher emerge from the ship with a pickaxe. He charged at the nearest drowned.

As Asher attacked one, Mason hit the others. He loaded his bow again and again, striking the drowned with arrows. *Thwack, thwack, thwack!* With a grunt, one went down.

Asher defeated his mob, too. As the mob gurgled and fell, something landed on the ground—a drop. And Asher was on it like an ocelot on fresh salmon.

He raised it up into the moonlight like a trophy. "A nautilus shell!" he cried out. But it was too soon to celebrate.

The third drowned came from out of nowhere. As it reached for Asher, its blue eyes glowed like an Enderman. But Asher was so busy admiring his nautilus shell, he didn't even know the drowned was there!

"Asher!" Mason cried. He couldn't fire an arrow—he'd risk hitting his brother. "Look out!"

Asher whirled around with his pickaxe, knocking the drowned backward. Then Mason aimed his bow and fired an arrow. *Thwack!*

Thwack, thwack!

After two more arrows and a whack from Asher's pickaxe, the mob grunted . . . and was gone.

While Asher collected the drops, Mason scanned the beach, his bow raised. He pictured the army of drowned he'd seen in front of Luna's home. Would they all follow the boys to the beach, one by one?

I don't have enough arrows! Mason realized. He dodged a pile of rotten flesh, wishing the drowned had dropped arrows or a trident instead—something useful.

Mason stared again at the pile of rotten flesh. Is this what he and Asher would have to eat tomorrow, when they had no other choice? He kicked at it with his boot. *Maybe. But not tonight.*

As rain began to fall, Mason sighed and led Asher back into the ship. His brother carried his precious nautilus shell.

But Mason carried only his bow.

* * *

"So Uncle Bart isn't coming back?" Asher kicked the toe of his shoe against the ship's rail.

The boys were standing on the stern of the ship at dawn, staring overboard. Two small burn piles smoldered near the water's edge, proving that another drowned had paid the boys a visit overnight.

"I don't think so," said Mason quietly. "It's just you and me now. But we're going to be okay." He said the words with confidence, but he wasn't sure he believed them.

We're back where we started, but worse, he realized. Mobs were spawning left and right. The ship was falling to pieces. They had no food. No friends. No plan. *No hope.*

Even Asher's mood seemed to have sunk like a shipwreck to the ocean floor.

Mason started to pace, just as he had a short day or two ago. He felt as if someone had used a command block and sent him and his brother back in time. As if they'd never visited Luna. As if it had all been a dream.

But more warped boards in the deck proved that time had passed. Mason stepped on a board, testing its strength.

He heard the creak of the strained wood.

And then the unmistakable *snap*.

Before he could reach out his hands to stop himself, Mason fell straight through the cracked wood. He hit the ground with a thud and a groan.

"Mason!" Asher's worried face appeared in the hole above. "Are you okay?"

"I don't know." Mason wiggled his fingers and toes. Then he saw the trickle of blood oozing from his ankle. "Just a scrape." He wiped his leg and then stood up slowly, taking a look around.

The cabin of the ship was dark and dusty. A cobweb stretched across one corner of the room. As Mason spun in a slow circle, he took it all in. Where was he?

Asher lowered himself through the hole. As his sneakers hit the floor, he sucked in his breath. "What room is this?"

Mason shrugged. "I don't know. I've never seen it before."

Uncle Bart's supply chest and furnace were below deck near the bow of the ship. But Mason had never seen what Bart kept in the stern, beyond the bedrooms. He reached for the door, wondering how this room connected to the others. But it was locked.

"A secret room!" Asher exclaimed. "Cool! What's in here? A treasure chest?"

Mason squinted into the darkness, trying to make out the blocky shape of a chest. But Asher found it first.

As they lifted the lid together, Mason held his breath. What would Uncle Bart hide from the boys that he didn't want them to see? It was like being back at Luna's house all over again.

He prepared himself to see the glitter of diamonds or gold. But the first thing he saw was paper—a stack of empty white sheets. Then a leather-bound journal. And an ocean explorer map.

Asher groaned. "It's a map chest," he said. "There's nothing special in here. We got our hopes up for nothing." He turned away in a huff of disappointment.

But Mason had already spotted something else—something familiar. The paper was folded in quarters, the creases heavy and worn. As Mason lifted the paper from the chest, his stomach clenched with realization.

He slowly unfolded the paper, already knowing what he would find.

Sure enough, it was Uncle Bart's buried treasure map.

The one that Luna *hadn't* stolen.

CHAPTER 14

"So she didn't steal Uncle Bart's map?" Asher asked again.

Mason shook his head sadly.

"But she did steal his helmet?"

Mason shrugged. "I don't know."

Ever since they'd found the buried treasure map, Mason had felt flat as a sail on a windless day. He didn't know what to think about Luna anymore—but she'd been telling the truth about the map. He knew that now.

Another moment of silence passed before Asher asked, "Do you think she's okay?"

"What do you mean?" Mason asked.

"Do you think the drowned got into her house?" Asher's eyes were wide with worry.

Mason shrugged. "Probably not. That's a pretty strong door—it keeps out the ocean, after all."

Asher hesitated. "Yeah, but . . . that door was open, remember? The drowned were already inside."

Mason's stomach dropped at the memory. Yes, a drowned had gotten into the first door. And there were so many more behind him—some carrying weapons. *Was* Luna okay?

"I bet Luna fought them off," he told Asher. "She's pretty tough." *But she's also all alone,* he thought to himself. *At least Asher and I have each other.*

To distract Asher, he opened the leather-bound journal they'd found in his uncle's chest. "See?" said Mason. "This is how Uncle Bart was going to build a conduit."

Seeing his uncle's scrawled handwriting made Mason's heart ache, so he focused on the drawings. "This crafting recipe shows that we need nine nautilus shells and a Heart of the Sea. If we can find those things someday, maybe we can craft the conduit ourselves."

Asher turned to face Mason. "You think so?"

Mason nodded. He'd say just about anything right now to make Asher feel better. But the truth was, they wouldn't be searching for the Heart of the Sea any time soon—not without food, or enchanted armor, or potions. Not without Luna.

As they stared out at the open water, Mason saw something darting in and out of the waves. A fish? No, a dolphin. "Asher, look!" As he pointed, more dolphins joined in the fun—five or six of them.

Asher watched in wonder. "There are so many," he said. "I wish there were that many of us."

Mason smiled. "Me, too. I'd feel safer that way."

"And we'd have a lot more fun," Asher added.

"Except . . . there'd be more of us to feed." His stomach growled, as if right on cue.

Mason sighed and asked the question he'd been asking for the last twenty-four hours straight. "Are you hungry enough to eat fish yet?"

Asher stared out at the open water. Then he smiled. "I have a better idea," he said, jumping to his feet.

A half hour later, Mason pulled a tray of crispy dried kelp out of the furnace. Asher had waded into the water and collected it himself. And it was delicious.

"The sea is loaded with this stuff," said Asher, talking with his mouth full. "We'll never run out of food again—thanks to Luna."

At the mention of her name, Mason's throat tightened. "You're right," he said. "She did help us." *And we accused her of being a liar and left her to fight off an army of drowned all on her own,* he thought to himself. He pushed away his plate.

Night was falling now, which meant it was time to light a torch and arm his bow. As Mason reached for the torch, he suddenly wished Luna were there too. They could take shifts, sleeping while the other kept watch. They'd be safer.

I wish there were that many of us, Asher had said, watching the dolphins.

Me, too, thought Mason. *Even three is better than two.*

But it was too late—too late in the day to waste time wishing, and too late to make things right with Luna.

As the sun disappeared over the horizon, Mason set up watch in the cracked hull of the ship. Asher soon fell asleep, his stomach full of kelp. So Mason waited on the mobs all alone.

* * *

Mason had stepped outside for only a moment. He had seen something glistening in the moonlight—something shiny in the sand.

Mason felt as if he were dreaming, except he hadn't slept a wink. What time was it? Two in the morning? Maybe three?

But that shiny drop called to him, so he stepped outside. He nudged the object with the end of his bow.

When he crouched beside it, he finally recognized the speckled shell of a turtle egg—a *cracked* turtle egg. And there was another nearby, smooshed and runny. Had a drowned stomped on them? Mason imagined how angry Luna would be if she were here.

Then he saw a third egg—shiny, round, and intact. He reached out to touch it, but then remembered Luna's warning. *Don't touch that!* So instead, he buried it safely in the sand.

As he smoothed the mound of sand, a shadow crossed his hand. Something was flying overhead. It veered in a circle around the beach.

Mason's blood ran cold. The phantom had spotted him from up above and was coming back for a closer look. And Mason sat in the middle of the beach like a stranded turtle—with nowhere to run.

He heard the flap of wings and felt a rush of cold air. As Mason ducked low, the phantom clipped his shoulder—a blow that sent him face-first into the sand. He rolled onto his back and angled his bow to take a shot.

Thwack! He hit the belly of the beast as it soared upward. It flashed red with rage, but didn't fall.

As the phantom rejoined the ring of mobs now circling the sky, Mason tried not to count. Five, maybe six—it didn't matter. He was outnumbered. He reached for another arrow.

As the next mob circled low, it hissed and darted toward his arm, nipping at his flesh. The bite stung—but Mason waved the beast off. He whacked it with his bow.

Now another mob was diving. And another!

Mason leaped to his feet and raced back toward the boat. But the bird-like beasts followed.

"No!" he cried, waving them off. Asher was sleeping inside the hull. Mason couldn't lead the phantoms straight to his brother. But what choice did he have?

He veered right, toward the water, hoping the move would throw the mobs off his trail.

But one mob followed. As Mason dove into the waves, the phantom was close behind. Mason hugged the sandy bottom of the beach, keeping his head low. He saw the tail feather of the beast cut through the water. And then it lifted again as the phantom flapped its broad wings and flew away.

Mason surfaced long enough to catch his breath and check the sky. The phantoms were still there, swooping lower. They could see him right through the water. *I can't escape!* he realized.

He couldn't lead the phantoms back to the ship, where Asher was sleeping.

He couldn't hide in the shallow waves.

And he couldn't breathe underwater for any longer.

So Mason gripped his bow, sprang from the waves, and prepared to fight.

CHAPTER 15

As Mason leaped from the waves, he released his bow skyward. But a phantom was already upon him.

The mob collided with his bow, cracking it in two, and then carried it away with a screech. For just a moment, Mason stared at his empty hands.

It's gone, he slowly realized. *I have nothing to fight with.*

He raised his hands in the air, as if giving up. Then he heard the cry—not of a hostile mob, but of a human.

Something silver slashed through the darkness near the edge of the beach. Was it a sword? No, it was bigger than that. A trident! But who was carrying it?

Mason wiped the water from his eyes and saw Asher charging a swooping phantom, swinging the trident wildly from side to side. "I'll cover you!" Asher cried again to Mason. "C'mon!"

When a beast flew low enough to attack, Asher leaped off the ground, swinging the trident. He whacked the beast's tail feather. The phantom grunted and wobbled upward into the night sky.

That's when Mason made a break for it, sprinting out of the shallow water toward the ship. As he ran, he saw Asher take another swing. This time, the phantom burst into flames. Asher pumped his fist. "Yes!"

But Mason knew that more phantoms would follow. "Back inside!" he called to Asher. "Hurry!"

As they darted back into the hull of the ship, Mason whirled around to guard the opening. But with what? Asher had the only weapon now. So Mason let his brother stand guard for the very first time.

Asher stared out into the darkness, gripping his trident. "Why did they spawn?" he asked Mason, trying to catch his breath.

"Because," said Mason. "I couldn't sleep. Luna says that when a phantom spawns, you've been awake too long." *And alone too long,* thought Mason.

Asher was beside him now—and somehow, without Mason even knowing it, his brother had become a fighter. *But there are still only two of us,* thought Mason. *It's not enough.*

That was when he made his decision.

* * *

They left the ship at daybreak. But this trip underwater to find Luna would be different. *Because we've learned a thing or two,* Mason realized.

Instead of swimming underwater, they paddled the

rowboat out to sea. Asher kept watch for the whirl-pool—the sign that the bubble column was down below. When he saw it, he waved his hand.

Mason stopped paddling and set the anchor. He reached for his turtle shell helmet and tossed one to Asher, too.

Then Asher grinned and reached under his seat for the bowl of suspicious stew. "Bottom's up!" he said to his brother. He plugged his nose with one hand and downed the stew with the other.

Sometimes when you take a risk, good things happen, thought Mason, remembering how fast Asher had raced around the deck after eating the suspicious stew. Hopefully it would help Asher swim faster, too. Mason crossed his fingers.

As soon as Asher set down the empty bowl, his leg started to bounce, eager to get going. "Ready?" he asked.

"Ready," said Mason. He made sure Uncle Bart's journal was tucked safely into his chestplate. Then he reached for the heavy trident. If the drowned were lingering below, Mason would be ready. And after seeing the way Asher had fought off the phantoms, he knew his brother could use the weapon, too.

Then together, they jumped. This time, as they swam to the bubble column below, Mason let Asher lead the way.

* * *

"You came back." Was Luna relieved or upset? Mason studied her face, but he couldn't tell.

They stood in her entryway on a soggy sponge mat, waiting for her to invite them in. But an awkward silence filled the air.

"Well, it wasn't easy to find your house," said Asher, chatting nervously. "Edward helped us."

They had run into the squid just outside the rocky ledge, and he had practically pointed toward the entrance with one of his sticky tentacles. *Funny,* thought Mason, *that I was ever afraid of a squid.*

Luna smiled at the mention of Edward, but only a little. She opened the door and let the boys inside.

Then it was Mason's turn to say something. But how should he start? He cleared his throat. "We just wanted to, um, make sure that you survived the drowned attack." He studied the glass walls of her home, as if checking for damage.

Luna jutted out her jaw. "Of course I did," she said. "I can take care of myself."

"Right," said Mason. He swallowed hard. "Well, we also wanted to say that we're sorry for calling you a liar. We found this when we went back to our ship." He slid Uncle Bart's folded map out of his chestplate and handed it to Luna. "I'm really sorry."

Luna's face softened as she glanced at the map. "It does kind of look like mine," she admitted. Then she took a deep breath. "I have something of yours, too."

She disappeared into the crafting room. When she came back out, she was holding Uncle Bart's helmet. She handed it to Mason, but she couldn't meet his gaze.

"I'm sorry," she said. "I found it on the ocean floor a few days ago. I should have showed it to you."

"Why didn't you?" asked Asher.

She threw out her hands. "Because you thought Uncle Bart was still down here hunting treasure! I didn't want you to give up hope of finding him." Her voice fell to a whisper. "I know what it's like to give up hope of finding the people you love."

Is she talking about her parents? Mason wondered. But there was no more time for secrets. He asked her outright. "Did you lose your parents, Luna?"

She hesitated, but finally nodded. "My parents had a kelp farm outside the village. I was exploring the reef one day about a year ago. When I got back to the farm, it had been destroyed by a drowned attack—I could see the drops everywhere! I knew my parents had fought. But there was no trace of them. They were just . . . gone."

Asher sucked in his breath. "You've been alone all this time?"

She cast him a sad smile. "I can take care of myself."

"Yes," said Mason, "but it's safer being together."

"And more fun," added Asher. "Like the dolphins." He grinned.

"Huh?" Luna wrinkled her brow.

"What we mean," explained Mason, "is that we have to trust other people and stick together. We're stronger together. So . . . what do you say, Luna? Do you want to help us find the Heart of the Sea and more nautilus shells? And maybe build a conduit one day?"

He slid Uncle Bart's journal from his chestplate again and handed it to Luna.

She barely looked at the pages. When she closed the book, her eyes were watery. "Yes," she said. "I really do." Then she waved them toward the crafting room. "C'mon, let me show you something."

This time, she threw the treasure chest open wide. The potion bottles, gold ingots, and emeralds had been pushed to the side to make room for nautilus shells—a *lot* of nautilus shells.

"Whoa," said Asher. "Where'd you get all those?"

Luna shrugged. "I fought off the drowned the other day. Like I say, I can take care of myself." She grinned. "But it'll be way more fun to fight off the drowned together."

As the smell of baked fish wafted into the room, Asher lifted his nose. "Is that dried kelp you're making?" he asked.

Luna caught Mason's eye and laughed. "Nope. It's something even better. Want to try some?"

No way, thought Mason. *Asher will never eat fish.*

But Asher shrugged and followed Luna out of the room. Mason shook his head and chuckled as he lowered the lid of the treasure chest.

"It's okay," called Luna from the hall. "Just leave it open."

So he did. No more secrets. No more hidden treasures. Except the ones they were going to find someday soon—together.